THE DEMETER DIARIES

BY MARGE SIMON AND BRYAN D. DIETRICH

ISBN: 978-88-31959-45-2

COPYRIGHT (EDITION) ©2019 INDEPENDENT LEGIONS PUBLISHING

COPYRIGHT (TEXT) ©2019 MARGE SIMON & BRYAN D. DIETRICH

OCTOBER 2019

PROOFREADING: MICHAEL BAILEY
COVER ART: WENDY SABER CORE
INTERIOR ILLUSTRATIONS: LUKE SPOONER

PRAISE FOR THE DEMETER DIARIES

"A cool and very creative interpretation of Bram Stoker's voyage of the Demeter."
—**Dacre Stoker**, great grand nephew of Bram Stoker, co-author of *Dracul.*

"What a wonderful idea for a poetry collection! Bryan Dietrich and Marge Simon have collaborated on The Demeter Diaries, a conversation in poetry between Mina and Vlad from Bram Stoker's Dracula. Vlad's lines are suitably tight, classical, the use of enjambment tightly locking the lines together and emphasizing Vlad's considered choice of words—after all, he's had a few extra decades to think about them. Mina's lines are long and prose-like, evoking her enthusiastic romanticism with a kind of breathlessness. It's well-suited to her part in this dramatic dialogue, allowing her to show off her lady's education and quote from her reading (in this case segments of the poetry of Keats and Poe). Simon and Dietrich appropriately end the sequence with two poems in parallel, with short lines from each alternating down the page as the lovers call and respond. An impressive collaboration."
—**Steve Rasnic Tem**, Multiple Stoker and International Horror Guild Author

"The Demeter Diaries is an intriguing retelling of *Dracula* in prose poetry form. Original, compelling, concise, and precise as one might suspect from two top notch poets. This is a must read for fans of the original novel. Highly recommended."
—**Gene O'Neill**, *The White Plague Chronicles*

"A wicked read: sensual, romantic, transgressive. Lovers dancing in a maelstrom of death and desire. This would be a great stage-play for the right two actors. They'd have to be very thin, the woman very young, the man brooding and handsome, both pale, with very red lips."
—**Mary Turzillo**, Nebula and Elgin winner, author of *Bonsai Babies.*

"Did you ever think that "Dracula" was a little biased against the vampires? And maybe if you heard the story from the other side, it might come out a little different? Well, Bryan Dietrich and Marge Simon show you the other side. And maybe it comes out a little different. I charge you: read this one, and find out."
—**Geoffrey A. Landis**, award-winning poet and science fiction writer

MARGE SIMON AND BRYAN D. DIETRICH

THE DEMETER DIARIES

INDEPENDENT LEGIONS

Mina: *I believe we should have shocked the 'New Woman' with our appetites.*
— *Dracula* 1897

Van Helsing: *We know how to save Miss Mina's soul if not her life.*
Vlad: *If she dies by day. But I shall see that she dies by night.*

— *Dracula* 1931

Van Helsing: *Now you're part of him, aren't you?*
Mina: *Yes.*
Van Helsing: *Can you tell me where that part is?*
Mina: *Darkness.*

— *Bram Stoker's Dracula* 1974

Vlad: *I have crossed oceans of time to find you.*

— *Bram Stoker's Dracula* 1992

Bryan:

For Marge Simon and Steve Lundin.

You helped me rise again.

Marge:

Dedicated to my kindred writers and poets who make

the Magic of literary darkness happen.

VLAD

I know nothing about you but your blood,
the porcelain price your neck pays to be
so fragile. No, that is a lie. I may suspect,
may conjure, but know? I know exactly
nothing, not even that incarnadine
dream. Nothing about you is incarnate
yet. Only the tin type, the oval within
an oval I have taken from he who came
here to help me acquire … things. He told
me of your betrothed, of you. He shared
the locket he stole for the silver. Coward,
money grubbing sycophant. Renfield
is as tasteless as his grubs. My other wives
find him mealy, gangly, too thin to waste
their grace on. As I prepare for you, to cross
oceans for you, to cross swords and time
and time's temple for you, I imagine
your fingernails at my ear, your voice, hot
at my artery, your fragrance trapped
on my tongue while my heart stutters
out its last long beats alone. Soon it will
share two tributaries, my Mina, soon
we will not *need* to bleed alone.

MINA

To the one who knows me as no other, or can it be a dream?—it has to be a dream— Still, I feel your presence with me ... Today something very odd happened. Jonathan had stopped by this afternoon to take me on a stroll; Father had interceded, inviting him to share a cigar in the study. I went into the parlor thinking to pass the time with a book. Instead, I found myself at the piano by habit. Usually I just play a few idle chords, these days. But this time, Ben Jonson's "Song to Celia" suddenly came into my mind! My fingers placed so on the keys as if by their own volition— surely you know the words—"Drink to me only with thine eyes ..." but when I came to this part:

The thirst, that from the soule doth rise,
Doth aske a drinke divine:
But might I of Jove's Nectar sup,
I would not change for thine.

These chords, those words, struck me so hard and sudden, I was quite faint for a moment. Then Jonathan entered the parlor. I sensed him there before I felt his hands over my eyes, as if a surprise. But he has no surprises for me. None that I readily want. Oh, I know you would understand. I know it surely as the beating of my heart. What is happening? Who are you, and where?

VLAD

Where am I? I have asked the night
that question. I have asked the creatures
who live there, so like me. I have asked
He who never listens, who unmoored me
from time. Oh, Mina, it is not a question
of where or when. I am *always*. My love
is always. It is a question of who. Who
am I? The owl, the bat, a plague of rats?
I am the one who loves you beyond this
body, beyond this bag of bereavement,
this husk of horror. I am far from you now,
across a sea as black as volcano glass,
but I am coming. I have been coming
ever since you left me. Since before I was
who I am now. Then, I could only imagine
death on a spit, my enemies skewered
like dead, red sweets. But now, lover,
now I penetrate more than skin and bone
and bowel. Now I enter their souls
as you have entered mine. You impale me,
Mina. *Me.* You slide through me like steel
or ironwood. You reach across the sea
with your soul and strike me as dead as I
have so long longed to be. You raise me
again in the blood of your being. You bleed

me as I long to bleed you. In a perfect world,
my love, we would walk between strange
saplings, twitching trees, the thorny thicket
of those I killed still waving their limbs. And we
would picnic there, in the shadow of death,
in the company of all I could not capture.
We would eat fruit there. We would eat rapture.

MINA

Do you call my name? But you *did*, I heard it clearly as I dozed. Awake now, I felt compelled to find you, to speak to you. Rising from my bed and drawing on my robe, I tip-toed downstairs to the patio. The evening was humid, heavy with perfume of lilac and honeysuckle.

Jonathan always brings a bouquet for me when he visits, but even the sweetest flowers lose their scent so quickly, or so it has seemed in recent days. What flower would you select for me?

Perhaps this part is from the dream or perhaps I confuse my real world with another, but I saw a shaft of moonlight cutting a swath though the garden. At its end, there was a single blood rose, strangely open this late and in full bloom. Drawn to its fragrance, I bent low to smell it. Then I saw its thorns were huge, almost as big as the rose itself and drew away. Just as I turned to go inside, I heard the flapping of wings. So near they came, I felt the wind of their passage. I supposed it was an owl or some strange bird of darkness.

It felt so right to be out there in the garden. The trees silhouetted below a gibbous moon. The quietude. It was as if I could almost hear your thoughts, and your desires must be mine as well. Longing for your touch, neither do I question why …

15

VLAD

Oh, my love, question everything, especially me.
Even as I go to prepare a place for you, for us,
I know my mansions mean less than salvation.
I would kill you now if I could. I would kill me.
I mean to be with you, to be all I can be for you,
but it will never be enough. There is no heart
in it. No soul. Flesh. Flesh is all I have to offer,
this dark meat and lasting supper. Hunger
I can provide. Longing and love I can promise.
But when the night nictates closed and my children
call, when the sweet music of madness makes us
walk the walls of your city searching for souls
we will never fully transubstantiate, *their* blood
will become *our* blood only briefly, their flesh
ours only a moment. Some say it is this way
for everyone, the body replacing its cells every
seven years, but we will be new each day, we will
have to be because I am so old. You too, are old,
a soul reborn, a face I could look upon a thousand
years at a sitting, but if I come, and I will, if I take
you, and I will, if you invite me inside you,
and you will, you will not know your soul again.
This is my doom. This, my dream. This, my darkest
damnation, like that ballad by Browning. I want
you for all eternity, my Mina, I want you beyond

what is right or just. I want you the way David must
have wanted the woman at her bath, the way Delilah
or Salome wanted their bucks. I am willing to go
anywhere, do anything, pull the stars down spinning
from their spheres, though the Earth crack and heaven
burn. I am willing to drown you, strangle you, eat you
even as Lycaon or Ugolino sated on their sons. I will
devour you as believers devour their god, and in me,
in you, we will transform each other, plague each other
every night, remembering the first flesh, the first
peach, the last garden we require to corrupt.

MINA

O love, these nights I find it increasingly impossible to sleep. Mama worries so. She says I've grown thin as wheat and summons Doctor Seward. He prescribes an opiate. The pills are small, easy to tuck them under my tongue and pretend to swallow. Sarah brings me hot chocolate and tea cakes fresh from Cook's oven, yet I've no appetite. How I wish they'd stop fussing over me. Only a few days, and they are so concerned! It's not food that I crave—I am consumed with passion for a man I've never met. I'd so like to confide these feelings with my dear friend Miss Lucy, but she is terribly unwell these days. Besides, it would never do for me to be unfaithful to Jonathan. I should feel such shame— and of course I would, if these recent fantasies were real. And yet, here I am telling *you* my feelings!

Tonight, I have Sarah draw my bath and dismiss her. I soak the sponge and let it linger in certain places as I wash. I imagine your hands caressing my skin, your lips between my thighs—I blush to think of such a thing! But it is true, I would deny you nothing. The bath salts turn the water the color of sweet grapes. I find this quite pleasing, for it matches the veins in my arms. The scent is hypnotic. I don't try to understand what this means, but it seems as if you are so close.

When I open the tallest windows in my room, the air is warm and moist, breathing on its own. I bite my lips into a shade you'd like, wipe away the drops.

VLAD

Oh to be a sponge, to be the water
you wade. I could bathe you my dear
in a tide not even Bathory imagined.
I knew her once, biblically, satanically.
Does this shock you, pale one? Does it
excite you? I have known many women,
many who adapted to my taste, but none,
my Mina, like you. You, I will not have
to teach. Elizabeth took months, Lucrezia
a bit longer, though the skills are simple.

Red ripples, red struggles, red bubbles
as the source grows silent and we lounge
together in the tub, slowly stroking each other
scarlet with tallow bars reduced from previous
playmates. I have a large hog scalder, iron,
clawfoot, so modern it easily fits three.

As I prepare for my departure, I see
your betrothed arrives in two moons.
Replacing Renfield no doubt. I will send
my tub back on the same wagon. It will arrive
at the dock, all prepped for exodus, around
the same time I am done with your man.
I promise to make him comfortable.

I promise to provide him consolation.
I will let my wives bathe him. Myself?
I leave soon. I will bring the soap.

MINA

Summer has arrived in its splendor. Oleander and bee orchid—such divine scents rejuvenate my soul! I've been most ill, but not of body. I tell myself it is the malady of guilt. Too many hours devoted to an incorporeal being I have never met. Poor Jonathan! I have put him through so much, trying to hide my uncertainty. How could I have been so uncaring of his attentions? He is a wonderful man, a Godly man. Father holds him in the highest regard and Mama showers him with attention during his visits. She makes sure he has his choice of teas—something she has never done for any of my suitors. She serves him fruity pastries, berries with a jar of clotted cream—how she fusses!

Mama is ever more concerned about my eating habits. She cannot understand that the sustenance I seek is not from food. Truly, I do not know what it is—only the fact that appetite eludes me. So I shall pretend to enjoy the soup tonight and eat a slice of bread. Whatever I must do to satisfy her, I'll try. My bedroom curtains are drawn tight, lest I be drawn again to venture in the gardens of the night.

VLAD

I have not felt you for weeks. I fear our connection
may be broken. I have worked more dark magics
than I can count. I have walked the wells of Derinkuyu,
the back alleys of Ubar and Thonis. I have desecrated
dozens in the Catacombe dei Cappuccini and sacrificed
singing girls in the Hoia-Baciu Forest. From the stones
of Altai to the blood waters of Rio Tinto, I have woven
hex lines and painted the lintels of a hundred thousand
homes with human blood, all to draw the not-yet-dead
to me.

But I cannot explain this empathy with you,
the spell you have snared me in, the tremors of your tears
throbbing through silk I never spun. It is not written,
though I write. It is not spoken, though I speak. How
can I know you when I have never met you? What dark
magic is Mina Murray? What glamour have you braided
between your standing stones and crossed bones, your chalk
horses and chalk men and exsanguinated scarlet women
spilt like tithes on the steps of your whitest chapel?
And how dare I try a counter conjuration?

I will not.
I will come to you, dearest, as I have come to you
so far. As mist. As a fever of the mind. I will sail
the sea in a closed coffin and rise and rise and rise
again until the decks are drowned in death. I will come
to you on a ship called the *Demeter*. I will be a ghost
in its bowels as you are a ghost in mine. I will descend
like the ship's herald herself, and in the land of unlikeness
I will seek my second soul, my reason for ruin, an end
to the end of the world.

MINA

I am distraught, my love, and ever more confused about my feelings. Some weeks ago, Jonathan had planned a trip for us—a brief stay at the Grand Hotel in Brighton, by the sea. Of course, it was to be with separate rooms and chaperoned by Auntie Maude. At first, I'd agreed to go—for in truth, I'd hoped I'd find your presence nearer, there by the great ocean. Yet soon I came to feel it will be even farther from you. I begged him to consider a stay on the eastern coast instead, but he will not hear of it. He said there's nothing on those shores but troubled skies— alliances, entanglements of such import that he would not discuss with me. When the time came, I feigned illness, so the trip had to be cancelled. He mentioned he'd be going abroad on business in the days to come. I know not why, but I knew it would bring me great relief. It was wrong of me to think that way, but my mind has been so clouded these past days.

We went for a long stroll all the way to the orchard. There, he took my hand and gazed into my eyes. "I'm leaving shortly, dearest," he said. "Keep me in your thoughts and prayers, for I love you dearly," he whispered, pressing sweet kisses on my fingers. Overwhelmed with guilt, I lay my head upon his shoulder. I promised myself then and there, I would allow no more thoughts of *you* to seep into my waking days. Of course, I cannot help what strange mischief *you* might conjure in my sleep

VLAD

The air is moist here, as are my eyes, looking, as they do
upon the last castle, last land, last loves I leave behind
for you. The moon is a scythe reaping stars, cleaving clouds
to let me see what I must lose to gain you. It doubles itself
in the waters that lap the prow of this ship, the half-lidded
beast of night, prone, nodding as I stalk the forecastle past
the shrouds. We are leaving at gloaming, as I asked, pushing
back from the dock, the Danube taking us into its open pulse.
Some nights from now, it will hemorrhage into the Black
Sea, and from there, dear Mina, another sea, another ocean,
too much dark wine between us. I feel chill. I *never* feel
chill. I have not eaten for weeks, feeding only on what little
I can divine of you across these deeps. I say "divine." That is you,
not I. And I know I should not be doing this. I should let you
live. But your song, your mind, Mina, it scrapes at my soul
like the scream of a sea witch, like the paws of wolves worrying
a shallow grave. I heard it from the moment I looked
upon your image, this tiny moon of metal I wear against
the cold, *between* cold and cold. I am colder than the ambient
air. I bring my own mist. So too my own soil and stone
and finally, finally dearest, my own myth. I fear it will begin
to pass among the crew soon enough. Thinking of you,
    dreaming
you there on the other side of this undulant abyss, brings back

my hunger. I will need something besides you to keep the chill
at bay. For now, I will need another body's borrowed breath,
someone besides my love to woo between waves, to love to
        death.

MINA

Months ago, I bade Jonathan goodbye. As he held me close one last time, I felt a sudden pang of great concern for him. Why should that be? Will something awful happen to him, something that would put his life in danger? I prayed not so. Yet watching as his ship took sail, I felt that horrid weight of guilt and worry lift. Since then, I've sensed your presence as strongly as before. Can this be true, that you are closer now, my love? I feel your cool lips on my neck, on places Jonathan has never been allowed.

Though it's early winter, I'm still drawn to wander the garden. I fancy I'm warmed by the smell of you, so different from any other. It is a strange musk, a perfume that suits you well.

Tonight there was a chill wind from the north. Moonlight laid a patterned spread of ghastly indefinables across the garden. Even the stone nymph on the fountain—my favorite one—even that innocent thing seemed altered. Its chubby marble face was in partial shadow, but the eyes seemed to follow me along the path. Then I noticed something in the icy water. To my horror, it was a dying sparrow, doubtless shot by some mischievous young boy. Its blood had turned the surface to swirls of garnet. If only I could have saved it, blown life back into the poor creature! I reported this to Mr. William and then took to my chambers.

Back in my room, I feel I should pray for Jonathan, even if it is already too late. The doctor's opiate is still on the nightstand. I shall take one with a sip of tea and swallow, for I need to block you from my mind this once, my love. Just this once.

VLAD

I, too, have seen dead sparrows floating in tears.
I have seen dyed pigeons, *dead* dyed pigeons
fall by the hundreds on the heads of a wedding
congregation. It was summer, and the bride
wanted something special, though not so special
as she received. The church attic had boiled them
before they could be released, and when the trap
doors in the ceiling opened, life encountered death
the same way a man walks home in devil's rain.

I have seen death in life and life in death.
I have been to circuses where an elephant
crushed a man's skull as if stepping on a bell
cap mushroom, where the high wire left only
one alive. I have watched seals suck down dogs
in tutus and dogs wrench the wrecked necks of ducks
until their entrails made new red rings for the clowns.
I like the circus. I like the ringmaster. I like the way
life takes a break and lets theater run the show.

I like every whip crack, every forced roar of lions
less tame than their masters imagine. I like my books
just the same. *Justine, Juliette, Isis Unveiled, Night*

Side of Nature, Descent of Man. When I suffer
I reread *The Monk.* When I dote on myself, *Leaves
of Grass.* When I seek more? Bruno's *opera omnia.*
I can only wonder what you seek, what you dote upon,
what beasts your books become. Do you love poetry
or pornography? Magic lantern or Grand Guignol?

Ah, Mina, I would take you to Ciniselli's circus
in St. Petersburg if I could, share sweet meats
at the *Théâtre du sang,* but I have yet to know you,
your taste. Do you prefer the sparrow or the tears,
the pigeon or the bride, the elephant or his step
stone? Shall we pine or dine with the Lobster
Boy? Should you shake for the shills, fall
for a freak, or marry the mad magician?
Do you think you could go for the juggler?

MINA

O Mystery Love—

Yesterday I walked in popcorn snow, puffy flakes that melted on my tongue. Evening came, a blinking ball of moonlight dancing in and out the clouds. As twilight fell upon the snowy statues in our garden, they took on shapes of exotic animals. It was as if a circus came to please my fantasies. I've never been to one. I was indeed enrapt!

Sunday morning we attended church in the carriage, despite the foul weather. I confess this to you—and only you, who understand. When the boys filed in to light the tapers, I fancied they were capering like clowns about the ring, and when the choir rose up with flapping sleeves so self-importantly, I could barely stifle giggles.

On bleak afternoons, I retire to our library. I've been reading too much folly, but I don't care, for I hate the politics of pompous men in government where women aren't allowed. I find the Romantic poets to my taste, particularly Keats. I've even copied this one down for my diary, for it speaks to me. I know not why.

This living hand, now warm and capable
Of earnest grasping, would, if it were cold
And in the icy silence of the tomb,
So haunt thy days and chill thy dreaming nights
That thou would wish thine own heart dry of blood
So in my veins red life might stream again,
And though be conscience-calm'd—see here it is—
I hold it toward you.

Last night, deep in slumber, I heard you speaking to me. But perhaps it was only the opiate pills that Doctor Seward still insists I take. The dreams ... they are horridly unseemly, yet they arouse me so. I touch myself—I feel such shame.

VLAD

We have spoken of sparrows and bees, roses
and bats. Of the walls we might find any of them
behind. But so little of what frightens you, all
of you, is ever actually interred there. No, as I
bide my time here, in the hold of this ship,
as I count down the days by how many seamen
I can reasonably invite to share my silence
before someone raises hew and cry; as, instead,
I slake my lust the way poor Renfield does,
dining on the aldermen of the abbey, the deacons
of the dump, priests of the privy, bishops
of every bloody bier, I join my flock in breaking
fast the way *they* do. I become their cardinal,
their appalling pope. I take them, ounce by ounce,
into my mouth and into my veins and they become
the blood and body that raises me. They may
scurry behind the walls of Westminster, mount
the gargoyles of Munster, but they are the secret
servants of you all. They have brought you both
providence and plague. They have crept along
the pulse of every breathing dream, but they are
more important than many a man. More fertile,
more fortuitous. Wherever Man has made his mark,

they roam. Behind the beams of every monument,
every mansion, every mausoleum beneath a house
beside a forest beyond a mist above some tarn.
They rustle you into place, providing immunity
and ossuary in equal measure. And here, I,
feeding on their generosity, feel small. Not because
I consume or kill, but because if life were different,
if the times had turned just one more turn before this
civilization of boats and bolts, I would have been
a Piper. I would have played such songs that even
they, grown grand and fat in your bohemian bowels,
would have listened and loved and followed me.
Under the mountain. Alongside your children.

MINA

My Unknown One, where are you now? I search my waking self to no avail—you have been so close with me for weeks—it is as if you have vanished. I hear rustling in the corners of my room. I'm afraid to look.

Such dreams I've had! Terrible, terrible dreams. I fear to sleep. The skies are overcast and dull, by day. Many nights I cannot see the moon, nor yet a single star. Our lovely garden is starkly barren, save for nocturnal creatures. If I'm up to sitting on a cold stone bench long enough, I can see their beady eyes glowing under the bushes. It is a different place, alive and not.

Mama persists in enticing me to eat. It's so hard for me to get even a morsel of meat into my mouth. But if it's not well-done, I manage a few bites. Mama noticed this and tonight, I was served a plate of raw liver. The smell was repugnant. I wouldn't touch the frightful thing—its color similar to Father Martin's mottled face when he starts bloviating about sin. Yet strangely, when I soaked up the bloodied juices with one of the cook's fresh rolls, I found it rather to my liking. Mama was pleased.

VLAD

We both go hungry, riding the sea swell
this world comes to us on with aught but wants.
Waves are nothing but that which was, a fell
echo of all that is no more, yet moves, yet haunts.
Demeter sought her daughter, famished for her peach.
So I seek you, as the tide the moon it cannot reach.

I hear hunger in the creaking quarter deck boards,
a rumble of starvation in the ice-laced wind
that makes a rimed harpsichord of shrouds,
so that everything—every rise, deep descent—
is nothing but agony, a groaning rope, a scrim
of sail made flesh. I imagine your skin

in the white of the forecastle's flibbering jib.
I dream you as gibbet, each cage bar a rib.

MINA

Mama tries to coax me into helping her with seasonal festivities, but I feel no joy this year. Darkness smothers me, and daylight only brings despair. I suffer such depression as never I've known. Surely poets are driven to such melancholia to serve their art, but I'm no poet.

Even the piano brings me no respite. It's unbearably tiresome in this dismal room. I take a small canvas out to the garden, to paint *en plein air*. I bring out only tubes of black & white to suit my mood.

Our elms are stark and leafless now, like masts of a ship without sails. The air is frightfully still, as if the garden holds its breath.

Where are you now, my One? Tell me, does the bird in winter sing of death?

VLAD

I dream you as gibbet, each cage bar a rib.
I want to sing inside you like your blood,
but fear I may have tainted that perfect flood
with a glut of me already. Every ebb
of scarlet too like the brackish basin
this hold has become, its dark cargo, me,
growing like black mold over Chinese tea,
curdling the crew, passing my pathogen.

I want to sing inside you the way the dead
sing inside the sea, the way the last red
owl glows within the trunk of the last blasted tree
in the last dying forest in the least eastern lea
of the land I have left like flesh on a thorn,
but fear my flame fades like fool's fire at morn.

MINA

I can't tell what is real from what is not. I feel suspended, locked in a state of mind. Even the smallest task seems impossibly difficult.

I know Mama has been hatching a way to cheer me up. I was right, because my cousins Oliver and Hammond called by today. They insisted I accompany them to London. The Smyth-Gordon's are giving a huge gala this Saturday night. There is to be a full orchestra with Strauss Jr. himself conducting.

Of course, I said I couldn't go. I've nothing to wear. But Mama has thought of everything. She brings out the posh frock that Father brought me back from Paris this summer. It is quite lovely, a certain shade of scarlet satin, trimmed with gold. But the waist is so small I still must hold my breath, even with the weight I've lost recently. I shall have to suffer being lashed inside that horrid corset first.

Forgive me, my Secret One. I would much prefer to wait here. How I long to know your voice within my soul once more—that with such wondrous passion, I be again consumed.

VLAD

My fear flames and fades like fool's fire at morn.
It races up my spine like St. Elmo chasing storm.

I have faced the beast of Athol and the beast of Gévaudan,
I have battled Ogopogo and the Chinese wild man,

but these days upon the ocean, the crossing of the deep,
has left me with no way to fight the fear that stops my sleep.

When boat left dock and wind met sail, I never thought to lose
your voice, your thoughts, your décolleté, oh, your very shoes.

I miss your mind as winter winds its way between the sails.
I would pay my soul to buy your sigh, even that which ails

my dreamer while she dreams, hoping she still dreams me
as I feed upon these salty boys who sail a salty sea.

Mina, I am famished for your fancy, each assumption.
You, my shrine, the only wine, make beauty of consumption.

MINA

The ball was an unforgettable affair. There was an ice sculpture of a naiad embracing a sea-dragon. Surrounding it was a sumptuous spread of delicious edibles and servants circulating with endless trays of champagne. Strauss's magnificent orchestra gave us waltzes until morning. As the last dance played, we were toasting to Jonathan's well-being. Just as the music died, Hammond's glass snapped and cut his hand. Crimson droplets in my crystal flute! I couldn't tear my eyes away. I took a sip.

Tonight it is raining. The sky is alive. Is it you who commands the drum rolls of thunder, sending your passion in flashes of light? From my window I can see our garden. The wind has risen, whipping the trees into a monstrous dance. Tonight, I shall welcome dreams. I will not take the pills. I'll pretend that you are near—I'm not afraid.

VLAD

My shrine? Wine, the beauty of consumption,
blood's bold signature on linen, divine unction,
the image of you convulsing, life's last auction
selling you to powers beyond even me, junction

of that world and this, the aurora borealis
of the afterworld, the ensconced lights of Dis
presiding over everything that I, that *I*, will miss.
How have you done this to me? No caress,

no tease, no touch, no naked meals at bath,
no pillow talk, no midnight walk, no swath
of bodies left along some highland road, no death
at all, only life, wind, tempest, the shibboleth

of two tormented souls torn by land and sea.
Two tormented souls well west of Galilee.

MINA

Only yesterday I fully realized I've had no word from Jonathan! I've been at the mercy of my own distractions. Yet to be honest, I know that's not true. How many days I've waited for a sign, a snippet of connection with you, my One! But alas, nothing. Perhaps this feeling was only a dream within a dream.

I must be too immersed in my own fantasies. I found Father's copy of *The Scarlet Letter* in the study. It suited my disconsolate mood. When I returned to my room, Sarah was there kneeling on the floor beside my escritoire. The winds had been so fierce today, the window latch had loosed on one side, and Jonathan's portrait lay shattered on the floor. While picking up the shards, she slashed her finger. I quickly drew it to my lips. A lick—a precious taste, before she pulled away.

VLAD

I

One tormented soul wails west of Galilee,
west of Gibraltar, screaming into the sea,
long past the Black, past Cyrene, Tripoli,
as the wind and I blow like blind banshee
and we crack open clouds, here to Innisfree,
and we murder the men where they stand on the lee
and we freeze them to marble, break them like scree,

and the wind and I howl over each crystaled bone,
over mouths frozen open like glass xylophones,
and the bodies as bass notes contribute deep tones
to the symphony growing from every groan
of the ship as it sails, crewless, lifeless, alone,
and I wander among the dead men like a Throne
cast down from the walls of a heaven of stone.

II

Cast down from the walls of my heaven like stone,
I trouble the waters, demand a cyclone.

The wind racks and cracks, making corpse cracker jacks
as the fog wraps its lacks in a brackish black flax

and the water surrenders to kraken-like temper
while timber remembers each horrid December

and breaks at the ribs, both foredeck and aft
as if I were God, god of love, god of craft,

but this craft does not matter, neither should I,
for I have become wholly wind, wholly eye,

and I move across ocean and island and coast
and I drown even more and I drink each a toast

from the salt and the blood and the foam and the spew,
from all that is left of this crystalline crew.

III

From all that is left, this crystal, my crew,
I draw forth the power of all that comes due
when silence turns violence. Nail, screw.

In the center of thunder and lightning and rain,
I open each wound, I let my heart drain
out into the maelstrom, the legerdemain

of what I had thought I was headed toward,
the woman who stains me like blood stains a sword,

and I watch as the hurricane spreads what I spored

and my blood reaches out, from Cádiz to Chios,
touching every bay of the Barbary Coast,
a dark incarnation, a whore's holy ghost.

I miss you, my Mina. I am my own hell.
I come to you hungry. I ride the sea swell.

MINA

I've been in such a temper! Is it the weather or the news? My monthly has come and gone, so it's not that. No, it is a terrible unease—perhaps a disease of the spirit. Things I read, or see, or do are churning in my head. Things I miss. *Where are you?*

At breakfast, Father read aloud that New Zealand has approved the woman's right to vote. He grunted in disgust. I couldn't speak it, but I was thinking *why not here*? Women are poets, writers, artists, teachers, doctors, and maybe someday we'll be soldiers. Yet most of us are treated like we are frail, too emptyheaded to rise to the heights of men in society. Only *you* are different, my One. I don't understand, but I know *you* would never treat me as simple-minded chattel. Jonathan wouldn't either. But he hasn't sent a word in days and days.

Adding to my frustration, I broke my beautiful hand mirror. It was an heirloom gifted to me on my sixteenth birthday. Mama will never forgive me. I picked the pieces up myself, not asking for Sarah's help. She looks at me so strangely since that day Jonathan's portrait shattered. And yes, there was the sweet taste of her blood. I must not think of it.

I'm sick of being cooped-up, sick of the cold weather—it's early October and winter is setting in too soon. I gathered my paints and selected a small canvas. Ignoring his grumbling, I had Mr. Motts saddle my mare. I rode her astride, heading eastward toward the sea. Wind at my back, what joy to free my hair from pins!

Of course, the sea is too far for an afternoon ride, so I reined in at the crest of a hill. I fancied the long grasses blowing were turbulent waves, a ship coming into port on the horizon. Yet after an hour, I lost patience and smeared the canvas with alizarin and ivory black. I blurred out the ship, the blue-gray waves, left not a trace. Maybe it's about Jonathan. Maybe it's *you.*

I cried part of the way back home, and then I was done. I don't care.

VLAD

Here, in the eye of the storm I have made,
I think I feel you once again. In the silence
at the center of this cataract, I think I hear
you. I pass east of the Bay of Biscay,
moving north in a death ship whose sole
cargo is mourning. A score of sailors
drained, maimed, vivisected. White men
never understand what it means to die.
Only the slaves remain. Tomorrow I will
set them adrift in some small coracle,
leave them their lives and their stories.

I know about being outside, looking in
on the "pure" who parade themselves,
praise their impenitent god, and serve
the roast goose. I know the urge to rebel.
Turner, Toussaint, Dessalines … I am not
them. But neither am I what I used to be.

I have paid for being what I was. I will pay
until I am no more, and when I finally cease,
there will be nothing but stain on canvas,
infinitely interpretable, a "portentous,

black mass, a nameless yeast. A boggy,
soggy, squitchy picture truly, enough
to drive a nervous man distracted."

That American madman has it right.
The center of us, the color out of space,
the thing we seek and serve and angle
against, that which we desire and destroy …
That is our end *and* beginning, a vast expanse,
a muslin sea where everything becomes
its opposite. Wind, whale, life, love, slave,
stone, star. The many stars. Nothing remains
the same the day our contract is complete.

MINA

"A cyclone!" The newspaper shakes in Father's hand. "A most astonishing fluke of weather for this time of year. It's in the Bay of Biscay, heading up the coast of northern France!" So imperious his tone, as if he were the God of Events. "Never before has there been such an unpredicted phenomenon! The fishermen say it came out of nowhere, and the waves are so high as to put in mind the very gates of hell."

The night previous, I'd dreamed about Winslow Homer's painting of a Negro chained to the floor of a small vessel during a terrible storm. Sharks are swarming in the bloodied waves. They seem almost close enough to reach the man. But in my dream, instead of the Negro on the ship, it was Jonathan. I awoke wondering what this dreadful vision could mean. At last I fell into a sound slumber and thought no more of it until later yesterday, chancing upon a collection by Edgar A. Poe in the study. I was quite amazed to stumble on these lines from "The City in the Sea":

I stand amid the roar
of a surf tormented shore

And I hold within my hand
Grains of the golden sand—
How few! yet how they creep
Through my fingers to the deep
While I weep—while I weep!
O God! can not I grasp
Them with a tighter clasp
O God! can I not save
One from the pitiless wave?
Is all that we see or seem
But a dream within a dream?

It seemed there was something terribly important in that stanza. I couldn't quite grasp what it was, but it seemed to me that I should.

But that was yesterday. Today, I am smiling to myself, for *you* are back with me! My recent painting is drying, but oils can take months. With the pigments applied so thickly, I wonder if it ever will dry. I've decided I rather like it. I think of presenting it to *you*, someday soon. I've titled it "Death of the Raven." It owes nothing to realism, or any other form of art I've ever seen. Yet truly, it speaks of my—dare I say of *our?*—unrequited passion.

I feel lightheaded, giddy as a schoolgirl after her first taste of wine. Someday we shall bathe in a tub of Father's finest. I choose the Madeira. Yes, we'll have it poured full to the brim. O, my One, I've missed you so!

VLAD

At last I come to you, passing nearer now.
At last I feel and hear and smell you again.
Yes, even your scent assails me across the sea.
If I were your hound I would know nothing of harts
or hills. I would seek only you forever.

I would tear you and bury you and dig you up
once more just to play pitch among your bones.
I could spend months on your thighs alone.
Worrying you, grinding away at every morsel,
baying at the moon for one last glimpse
of the lap I would die to lay me down upon.

But some nights, some of these terrible nights,
sailing ever closer, I fear I have ushered in a tell-tale
mistake. The ship, the crew, this emaciated body,
its captain broken, wracked, strapped to the wheel …
None of this is meant for you. Hounds are not for you.

Ravens and rats and the night's own wings are not,
should not, serve my Mina. I fear all I have already
delivered to your dock. I worry the sails are set
on sorrow and tack toward endings, not beginnings.

I would that I could change the sextant, the stars
themselves. I would that I could sink alon

57

MINA

O love, I sense you're ever closer! We were at dinner when I suddenly felt your presence. I trembled so, I tipped my wine glass over. Old Dodson caught it before it hit the floor. He set down his serving tray and took my arm to steady me as I rose. Sarah came quickly to my side to escort me to my chambers. It was all I could to convince Mama that I didn't have the need for Dr. Seward. I told her I was having a difficult monthly and wasn't feeling well, but I think she didn't quite believe me. "You appear to be having one too many monthlies," she said, with raised eyebrow. But she left me be.

There is no way to describe the sensations I feel now—a delicious overwhelming passion, a relentless hunger as I've never known before. This unseemly obsession I embrace, pushing my hand down to my private place, rotating my fingers slowly, feeling the throbbing wetness rise. I lift to move with it, oh! My heart races, I am bleeding tears. And more, much more—I cannot speak of it. Even now, even to you, my mystery One.

VLAD

I have passed Brest and am deep in your Channel
now. I can taste you. When the natural winds
die, I summon great clouds of *Diaemus youngi*,
my white-winged children, to seed the sails
with all they know of the air, and we move on,
always on, toward you, my love, though I grow
maudlin of late, here among my only real kin.
I listen to their songs. I listen to all they scry
as they serve. They do not make me feel less alone.

I imagine myself your master, which I do not want.
I imagine you my slave, which I do not want.
I imagine finding you, touching you, having
to set you free on some small coracle.

You taste of salt now. And ash. You taste the way
I imagine Aphrodite did as she washed ashore
at her nascence, naked, born of bits of her father,
born of blood and brine. Is love *truly* the child
of death? Is this what happens when we murder
the sky, when time takes its taste of our flesh?
Chronos had to win. Sky is not enough. But why
anything else? Why do we inhabit space, time?
Why care if anything *ever* arrives out of the sea?

MINA

This morning at breakfast, I forced myself to eat a scone, heaping it with strawberry jam. I knew Father was watching me. He folded his napkin, smiling. "Pleased to see you're looking well today, my dear. It appears that I'm to make a brief jaunt to Darbyville to discuss the sale of some property we can do without. Would you like to accompany me there? The shops are quaint and offer bobbles women like. I think you will enjoy perusing them while I meet with Mr. Bracegirdle."

Indeed, I was overjoyed for a release from these walls. As the carriage jogged along, Father reached over to take my hands. "I'm most pleased you came with me, my dear," he said. "This business about Jonathan's absence—not to mention his lack of communication—has disturbed us all." He looked closely at my face. "I'm aware that your malaise is caused by deep concern for your intended. It breaks my heart that I cannot provide any answers." He went on to explain that his inquiries about Jonathan had been to no avail. He'd thought perhaps Jonathan's ship had foundered en route back. He did find mention of a missing vessel, the *Demeter*. Apparently, it had not yet arrived on schedule. A recent sighting of it by French sailors was the only thing on record. Curiously, it had strayed from its original course, but the sails were at full furl, and nothing about it seemed amiss. It was assumed that the captain had received a change of orders at some port en route.

My One, I wasn't even thinking about Jonathan while he spoke. We drove on in silence until something very odd happened. A sudden burst of lightning split the skies all around our carriage. It was inexplicable, for the bolts came straight out of a cloudless blue sky! The horses spooked and the carriage bounced around, half on and half off the road. I must have hit my head on the window frame because I can't remember a thing until I awoke on a settee. Father was administering smelling salts. A sweet old lady hovered near, and once I was awake, insisted I take a sip of brandy as a restorative. My temple was sore, but I assured them both I was feeling better and urged him to continue with his business.

Outside, I sensed your salty breath upon the wind, by far a more restorative than brandy. Had I my way, I'd take the carriage onward to the sea. I crave something new, something more powerful. The taste of blood on my tongue. You.

VLAD

I am almost upon you, my love.
The North Sea, long past the city
of Diss. Climbing the spine
of all you imagine modern.

I thought to land in London,
but I feel you farther north,
bedded deeper in frost. It is
almost the day of All Souls.

As I watch cadaverous cliffs
and green vales peek and perish
through these clouds that cover you,
your land, I think of Pergamum,

Pandaemonium, Kunlun,
Callanish. I think of the mist
rising from your thighs. Every secret
site a demon might call home.

MINA

O love, such excitement throbs with every heartbeat! I wait each day, impatient—I can't fathom this irrational belief, but soon I am sure I shall know.

Some days ago, while Father continued his business in Darbyville, I determined to keep occupied. Thankfully, I felt much more myself once outside. Why even bother saying that? Of course, I felt better, with your scent in the icy winds. I passed from shop to shop—hatteries and jewelers, fashionable frocks, imports. None tempted more than a passing through until I came to the last, almost hidden by trees. A sign above the broken fence proclaimed "Curiosities." At my knock, a tall young woman dressed in black answered the door. I found myself asking if she might have something unique—a gift for a lover returning from a long voyage at sea. She gestured to a glass case near the back of the room. "That one might hold something of interest for you. I wish I could be of more help, but Grandmamma is no longer with us. You see, I came here to tend her in her last months, and I'll be closing the shop in the next few months."

At the back of the case, I spied something half hidden. Once taken out into the light, I saw it was a smallish black leather pouch, certainly not of the sort a lady would have use. It appeared to be made of some odd animal skin, quite like that of a bat—the one that our gardener killed when I was a child. He showed it to me, and I ran my hand over the wings. Mama saw us and I was scolded for touching such a "filthy beastie." I never forgot that instant shiver of delight, touching it. Yet here it was again, that same feeling. Impulsively, I asked the price, and finding that I had enough coin, purchased it. The lady hesitated as she wrapped the pouch. "I just remembered something Grandmama told me about this pouch. I believe I should tell you that it came from Transylvania, wherever that is. She instructed me to share this information with the buyer, should anyone wish to purchase it. I daresay she seemed unusually nervous about saying more." You shall have it when we meet, my special gift for you within. Please, my Secret One—I pray it may be soon!

VLAD

Once upon a time, Darkness came from darkness
to take a lover, a girl picking periwinkle in a field.
Darkness arrived in his black hack. Dire dragons
breathed. The girl held her breath. Nature herself shook

when she found her daughter gone. Deserts cracked
black into greenswards. Forests fell fallow. Every crop
failed. As Nature wandered the wasteland she'd created,
immune to the moans of humanity, she thought,

I suffer. So should they. When she found her daughter
at last, lip-locked and love-lost in the arms of Darkness,
she made a bargain. She made Winter. She made a space
where death might live and not be ruled by Darkness.

I offer you that as I arrive, my love. Just that. Whitby
rises over the crest of the next last wave. You appear
in a field of periwinkle. Nature is nowhere here, not now,
but I am. I am here, at last. And I bring pomegranates.

MINA

This afternoon I informed Sarah I was resting and not to be disturbed. Alone in my room, I locked the door. I spread a washcloth on my desk, placing a sheet of stationary nearby. Earlier today, I'd borrowed a penknife from Mr. William, saying I wanted to try my hand at soap carving. Hearing this, he gave me one of his rare smiles and bade me to keep it, as his own daughter enjoyed creating animal likenesses in soap. I lit a candle and held the blade over it until I was satisfied it was clean, then quickly made a cut. I wasn't expecting so much blood so fast, but the small dish I'd pilfered from Cook was for that purpose. When this was done, I bound a handkerchief tightly over the wound.

I took up my pen, dipped it in the bowl.

darkest of dark
reddest of red
my love eternal

When it dried, I folded the note and tucked it in the pouch.

At dinner, Father produced a letter from the Westenras of Whitby. It appears that sweet Lucy has urgent need of my company at Prosper Hill. Though I am concerned for my dear friend, I am excited about a train ride north to the sea. Even more exciting, I've a suddenly strong feeling you'll be nearby, my One. How can I be so certain? How dare I hope?

VLAD

The ship has found harbor, Mina, the captain
his flock. The crew, dead, dreaming, still go
sailing round this deathless rock. Oh, England,
I have landed. What soil you do not have, I have
brought with me, dirt of my doing and undoing.

My rats have begun the invasion, staking claim
to all dark corners we need. Soon, I will hire men,
sullen, Jack London men, to bring me to the abbey,
to plant me so the two of us might blossom. Here,
in Whitby, there is a space yet between excess

and innocence. I feel there is one close
to you, closer to me. I will need her soon,
but fear not, my love. I did not spend this dark
passage reading the stories I spilled on the walls
only to fall for a poorer shadow of you. Mina,

now that I have come, now that I know the dead
better than I thought … Everything you love?
I know to *not.* You should warn her, your friend.
You should try. But remember, you are eternal.
Or will be, once I feed on what I need not to die.

MINA

Well before sunrise, my carriage arrived at the train station. I have my gift for you in a secret pocket of my cloak. As I was packing to leave, I noticed I still had the gifted knife in a drawer. Remembering passengers are often targets of robbers, I placed it in my toiletry case. Of course I am concerned for Lucy's wellbeing. Yet I am possessed by an ever increasing surety that I'll be seeing you very soon. I shall know the color of your eyes, the taste of you, but I must not think on that.

The ride was uneventful; I dozed as the car rocked back and forth. I dreamed I was in a topiary, arm in arm with Lucy. The bushes were quite strangely cut in shapes of fauns and vermin. Suddenly, she turned to me, her face a mask of hatred! I awoke, filled with great fear.

Thankfully, we arrived in Whitby soon after. Lucy was at the station with her father to greet me, looking as lovely as ever. How I envied her beauty! Her red curls were tucked into a hat of soft beige fur. Her skin was flawless, her lips red without the need of rouge. We embraced as old friends. Strolling to the waiting carriage, we shared the usual girlish greetings, yet I was still troubled and confided my dream. "You must think me silly," I said, "but I am in need of reassurance that all is well, dear friend." At this, her mouth drew back in a snarl, so like my dream. Her eyes narrowed as she pulled off her glove and took my hand in hers. It was cold and marked with broken veins. I held hers up to warm it with my breath, but dropped it instantly, for on her skin was a familiar smell. The same carried by an eastern wind on nights I strolled the garden. It was you, my One, it was your musk!

VLAD

I am tired of sea salt, of boys
too green to taste. I am weak.

So much blood and magic spilled
to get here, to be all you dreamed
me into being. Too little
of the old strength left in this soil
where I need you, Mina, the life
you promise, to save me, restart
my heartlessness. No, I cannot die,
but I can diminish, wither, lose
the flame and leave only wick,
as shrunken and shriveled
as the captain of the Demeter
racked on his ghost ship's wheel.

I have had too much time to think,
Love, too little distance between
what I am and what I must be.
A wolf cornered in a cave
with all his kills. A bat slamming
into skylights of the slaughterhouse.
Ahab lashed to his dying god.
I become what I arrived in,

an empty vessel whose manifest
lists only guilt, heavy hecatombs
of that, but no shame.
I have had your Lucy.

MINA

The rest of my arrival is a blur in my mind. I was deeply shocked and confused at Lucy's strange behavior. That scent—*yours!*—on her hand, I felt faint. We said no more until arriving at the Westenra's. All traces of that hateful look were gone from her face, replaced instead by a sweet smile. Her parents welcomed me most warmly and I was soon settled before a fire. Tea was soon to follow.

I must have been a fright, considering my agitated state of mind. Mr. Westenra noted my pallor and poured me a small glass of spirits. I'm not used to drink, and this was particularly strong whisky. Perhaps he'd added a dash of sedative to it, I don't know. But I soon felt very drowsy. "Sweet Mina, you must be fatigued from your long journey," he said. "Lucy, show Mina her room—you girls will have time to chat later. Have a good rest before dinner, my dear."

I must have slept hours. When I woke, I saw my cloak draped across a chair by the bed. The seams of the pockets appeared to be torn out. Your gift with my special note to you was gone! A knock came on my door. It was Lucy, her eyes were veiled and she wouldn't look at me. "Father wishes to speak with you in the drawing room, Mina. You must go see him immediately."

This cold young woman couldn't be my Lucy. I just couldn't believe it. Nonetheless, I checked my appearance, smoothed my dress and was soon before her father. He had his back to me, staring out the window. It was snowing. Nightfall would be soon. I cleared my throat. He turned to me, scowling. In his hand was the note I'd written you.

"Did you write this, young lady? Lucy says it fell out of your cloak. She was terribly upset, for it appears to be written in blood, so she brought it straight to me."

"This," he stepped closer, shaking it in my face, "this is a letter to a lover. Need I remind you of your pledge to Jonathan? Have you lost your virtue to a stranger?"

I had no words. I couldn't speak. I fled to my room in tears and locked the door. I had only one thought, that Lucy had betrayed us! *You are so near—I know you are, my One! Where are you? What is keeping us apart? I fear I am losing my mind!*

VLAD

Do not go looking for Lucy's father.
He came looking for me. It is the curse
of the sleepwalker that they know not
the road they somnambulate. The poor man

thought he could steal from you, from me.
Your smell was all over him. Your gift
was in his pocket. His head is in the abbey.
Other bits may be found here, there.

I left you my own valentine, Dearest,
as I flew with him over Yorkshire,
letting him ebb like the river Esk.
He was very gracious about it all,

his blood drizzling down on wold
and wainscot. With my ancient fist
for letters I have signed this mist,
the land itself. I know what is mine.

D.

MINA

I stayed in my room the rest of the day and into the night. It seemed strange that no one came knocking on my door, not even the maid. Mr. Westenra was so angry, I felt sure he wasn't finished upbraiding me. The skies grew dark, and darker still. A great wind rose, rattling the panes and shutters in a most alarming way. I fancied I could hear the moaning of lost souls, but there was no sign of a blizzard when I drew the drapes. It was then I sensed your presence, my One—even stronger than before. And you are very near, at last!

VLAD

I have stood beside you for nights now,
just this side of the pane. My indiscreet
anger brought priests to protect you
and your friend. Priests, doctors, experts.
Texas toadies. Lords of nothing. Even
my old nemesis, Abraham. They tend
to Lucy. They dote on your future.
They know nothing of sickness, nothing
about the future. The days that lie
before us stretch out in infinite sheets,
billow like sails, stain like bridal bed
linen. They fold. They grow old and yellow.
You must use them before they tatter.
Nothing sadder than a bed made for no
one. Nothing darker than the perfect
corner left unturned. I want so badly,
Mina, to join you now, to pass this
glass and guide you to the mountain
upon which desire's deity has bid me
slay you, lead you to the stone cairn
where both of us shall be altered, born
again. But the thorns of this life, the men
like Abraham who surround you, keep

me at bay. They make plans. They seek
my secret soil. Already they make it hard
to keep our sacred sickness from spreading.
Already, these men deny the sacrifice
that their gods, that we, demand.

MINA

It's been four days—maybe more, I've lost track of time. They keep me here, locked in for my saftey, as if a cloistered nun. But I am no bride of Jesus! I am in love beyond my senses. My chambermaid, Tandy, confides that Mr. Westenra has disappeared. Understandably, Miss Lucy has been confined as well, but I'm not allowed to visit her. I am brought meals, but I can't bring myself to eat more than a bite of bread, a sip of broth. I know only that there are men here with big voices. Tandy has obliged me enough to say that one is an officer of the constabulary and the others—she doesn't know. And there is that priest, Father Whittaker. He visited me yesterday with another man. This man speaks with a strong accent; I'm guessing it's German. His name is Van Helsing and his questions are many. He seeks to probe my most private feelings. Of course, I cannot answer for fear he will have me put away. Yet through all this, I am comforted by the nearness of you. I feign having the vapors and they leave me, but I know my tactics will not last. This morning, Tandy informed me that Dr. Seward is on his way. I know he will see right through any ruse I might pretend. The good Father has given me a Bible. He has little pig eyes and smells of camphor. I despise him. I spend afternoons on the chaise staring at the wallpaper. Flowery designs with signs of water damage. I fancy they are dripping tears of blood.

VLAD

The doctor tasted like poppies.
The priest like something un-urned.
The rest had a bouquet of Stilton.
But the Texan? A little bit burned.

I had thought *this* was the battle.
The final. Your end. Our escape.
But Abraham came and absconded
with you buried under his cape.

I turned to my friends in the sewers,
to my friends in the forest and skies.
The rumors suggest you head southward,
toward the great fjord of lies.

But London will not be our parting.
That madman will not have his day.
Those glaciers of stone and story
cannot keep your lover away.

I know this Van Helsing, his thinking.
It is all about apple and bite.
I suspect he is staging our end days
at an altar, a chapel, all white

MINA

Last night I sat at the window with the curtain's half drawn. It was almost midnight, and they'd turned off the gaslights, save for a few in the halls and one at the entrance. Out there, the shadows flicker-played their games of life and death. I felt your breath on my shoulder, your lips on mine.

But this morning, Tandy came with dire news. Her hands trembled and her face was flushed. "Mr. Van Helsing wants you. I'm to help gather your things. He said something about a trip to London. He … he is very demanding." I tried to calm her to no avail. So we gathered my garments. Though doubtful it would be of much use, I tucked the small knife in my pocket. In a way, I was all too glad to leave, but I didn't want to leave with this strange and rather nasty man who would be taking me farther from you, my One.

I have no choice.

VLAD

I have relearned mortality today, the prose the body knows. Eternity does not care for character, nor clarity, nor plot. When he took you, Mina, I realized just how long I have been away from the world, so much longer than I thought. What happens to you matters. What happens in this world of matter matters. There are graces *less* divine than poetry, *more* divine than philosophy, moments that drop upon our plates, that echo inside the ribwork of bled brigantines, that find themselves in our handbags or our hearts. They say attend. They say live. Alas, I cannot. Poetry is, by definition, undead. But what am I, if I cannot change? What is poetry if it cannot expand the universe? I have to be immortal to save you for death. I have to be mortal to bring you back to life. I am as sure as caesura, as amazed as metaphor, as I rush to your side, as I sweep in above all the clod hawkers and boozy buskers, all the leather stretchers lashed to pews inside this dread box he brought you to to die in. He wants to make a statement, prove a point, show fealty to an idea above me. He wants you as the lamb only *God* should provide. I have other plans. I have infinite bushes of thorns. I watch him strap you to the altar. I watch him remove his athame. My flying friends fill the belfry. My mewing minions fill the walls. Wolves stalk the street between this pale, pale chapel and Ten Bells. Nothing tonight will leave here alive. I think of Isaac, of Jephthah's daughter. I think of Medea's children, Jack's Jezebels, Philomel's savory sweets. I think how hot Abraham's blood will be by the time I reach his neck.

MINA

This madman, this Mr. Van Helsing! I beg him to tell me where we are going, but he clenches his jaw and stares ahead. Wherever in London is he taking me? It's nearing dark when we arrive, but I believe it's St. Mary Malfelon's parish in Whitechapel. I recognize a few buildings and street names.

He is no gentleman, his grip is harsh and hurts my arm. Abruptly, he pulls me out of the carriage and half drags me to the entrance. When I beg him to slow down, he turns to look at me. He doesn't speak. His eyes are glazed with hatred, but what have I done to deserve it?

I scream in protest when he lifts me up and lays me on the altar, preparing to tie me down.

No! I shall not go meekly to my death! I plunge my hand into the pocket of my dress and find the knife. Grasping it, I slash out and up with all my strength, aiming at what's closest—that precious thing between his legs, now pulsing with excitement through the cloth of his britches. He shrieks and drops his athame. With a second slash, I drive it deep into his throat and his cries become a gurgle. Such beauty in that bright wet flow!

Now I look up and see you high above me in the rafters. Of a sudden, you're beside me, your sweet lips on my neck, my shoulders.

In your arms at last, I swoon.

VLAD MINA

I was right about your purity.

O, my love.

Tonight I saw you seethe acetylene.

That final blow was up to me.

You lay me low with what you can do.

I've been so meek so long.

I was meek once too, lost, unforgiven.

Now you must hold me.

You reek of desire, your blood, his …

Yes, my One—on my skin, in my hair!

The spoil of the kill.

My garments stained—

A grand systolic canvas.

I must be clean for you.

We will make our own Godliness.

There has to be a tub within these walls.

Yes, behind the abandoned baptismal.

Help me to wash this filth away!

Here, I have soap—and, look, Lucy!

To serve?

To anoint.

Shall she draw our bath?

Yes, as you from Abraham's artery.

We should be rid of what's left of him.

We must move beyond the altar.

This soap, so odd, so divine.

Touch me.

Here, let me undo you.

Yes, take me.

Feed. Oh ...

Till we …

    We are both …

Oh …

    Oh, my One …

Both …

    Undone.

ABOUT THE AUTHORS

MARGE SIMON lives in Ocala FL. She is a retired art teacher with an MA in Fine Arts and a minor in English Lit from the University of Northern Colorado. Her fiction and/or poetry has appeared in Asimov's, Daily Science Fiction, Bete Noire, New Myths, and Polu Texni. Her works may be found in anthologies such as Tales of the Lake 5, Chiral Mad 4, You, Human and The Beauty of Death. Marge has won the Bram Stoker Award, the Rhysling, Elgin, Dwarf Stars and Strange Horizons Readers' Awards; she serves on the HWA Board of Trustees, maintains a newsletter column, Blood & Spades. Marge is the second woman to be acknowledged as a Grand Master Poet of the SFPA, and is on the board of the Speculative Literary Foundation. She attends the ICFA annually as a guest.

Website: www.margesimon.com

MARGE SIMON

THE
DEMETER
DIARIES

BRYAN D. DIETRICH is the author of seven books of poems and co-editor of an anthology of superhero poetry. He has published poems in Asimov's, Weird Tales, Strange Horizons, The New Yorker, The Nation, Poetry, Ploughshares, The Paris Review, and many other journals. He has won the Asimov's Reader's Choice Award, The Paris Review Prize, a "Discovery"/The Nation Award, a Writers at Work Fellowship, and has been nominated for both the Pushcart and the Pulitzer. Former President of the Science Fiction & Fantasy Poetry Association, Bryan is Professor of English and Chair of the Division of Arts & Letters at Newman University in Wichita, Kansas. He is currently co-writing a book of science fiction poems with the author Steven Erikson.
Website: www.bryandietrich.com

BRYAN D. DIETRICH

THE DEMETER DIARIES

INDEPENDENT
LEGIONS

THE MAN WHO ESCAPED THIS STORY AND OTHER STORIES
BY CODY GOODFELLOW

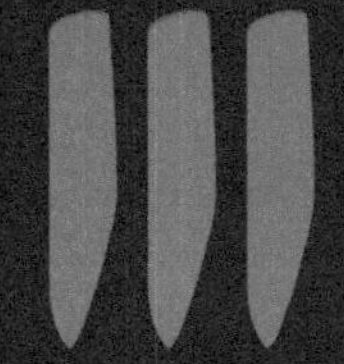

CROTA
BY OWL GOINGBACK

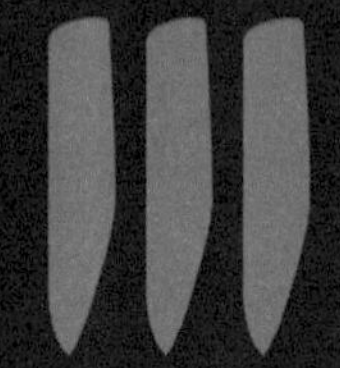

CALCUTTA HORROR
GRAPHIC NOVEL

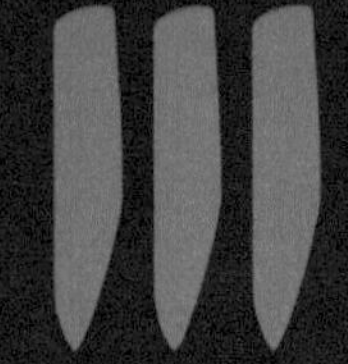

LATEST RELEASE

FEARFUL SYMMETRIES
BY TOM MONTELEONE

NARAKA
BY ALESSANDRO MANZETTI

LATEST RELEASE

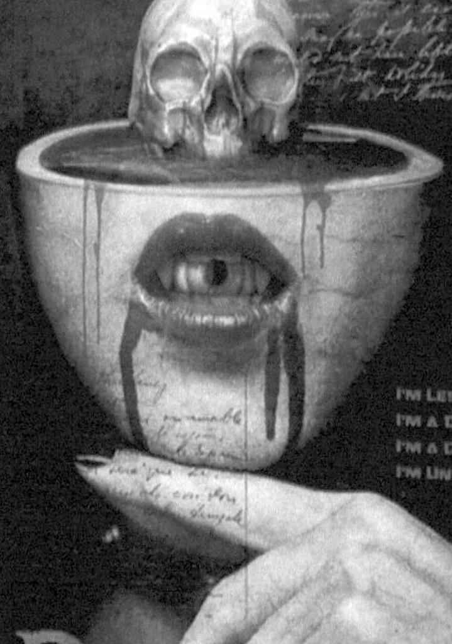

DARK MARY
BY PAOLO DI ORAZIO

AVAILABLE BOOKS

Our publications are available at Amazon and major online booksellers. Visit our Website: **www.independentlegions.com**

BOTH PAPERBACK & DIGITAL PUBLICATIONS

THE MAN WHO ESCAPED THIS STORY AND OTHER STORIES
by Cody Goodfellow

CROTA
by Owl Goingback

DARK CARNIVAL
by Joanna Parypinski

HORROR CALCUTTA (GRAPHIC NOVEL)
by Alessandro Manzetti & Stefano Cardoselli

COYOTE RAGE
by Owl Goingback

FEARFUL SYMMETRIES
by Thomas F. Monteleone

DARK MARY
by Paolo Di Orazio

TRIBAL SCREAMS
by Owl Goingback

ALL AMERICAN HORROR OF THE 21ST CENTURY: THE FIRST DECADE
Edited by Mort Castle

BENEATH THE NIGHT
by Greg Gifune

SELECTED STORIES
by Nate Southard

DIGITAL PUBLICATIONS

TALKING IN THE DARK
by Dennis Etchison

THE BEAUTY OF DEATH VOL. 1
Edited by Alessandro Manzetti

THE HORROR SHOW
by Poppy Z. Brite

DOCTOR BRITE
by Poppy Z. Brite

USED STORIES
by Poppy Z. Brite

THE CRYSTAL EMPIRE
by Poppy Z. Brite

SELECTED STORIES
by Poppy Z. Brite

THE USHERS
by Edward Lee

INDEPENDENT LEGIONS PUBLISHING
Via Virgilio, 10 – TRIESTE (ITALY)
+39 040 9776602

WWW.INDEPENDENTLEGIONS.COM
WWW.FACEBOOK.COM/INDEPENDENTLEGIONS
INDEPENDENT.LEGIONS@AOL.COM

www.ingramcontent.com/pod-product-compliance
Lightning Source LLC
LaVergne TN
LVHW051448170726
843492LV00002B/592